THE YEAR OF PENNY

Laurie Pluimer

Illustrated by Ethan Pluimer

PUBLISHER'S NOTE

This is a work of fiction. All names, characters, places, and
Events are the work of the author's imagination. Any resemblance
to real persons, places, or events is coincidental.
Cover art credited to Vecteezy.com

ISBN 13: 979-8-218-21941-3

Pecan Springs Publishing
https://pecanspringspublishing.com

For Mark,

our protector and provider, who carries us,

and for Ethan and Esther, our gifts beyond measure,

who fill our cup to overflowing.

CONTENTS

~One~

THE YEAR OF PENNY

So far, 1986 has been less than perfect. But it's a new school year, and I have a goal: popularity. I turned nine last May, so in eight months I'll be ten, double digits! I live with my mom, Dad, and the daily regret of a home perm.

One day during the summer, my hair decided to morph into a frizzy orb. It happened the day I joined my mom and my aunt on their weekly trip to the drugstore where they drink sodas and "discuss things." Gossiping is more like it.

I sat at the counter, thoroughly enjoying my cherry phosphate, when Auntie Anne noticed home perms were on sale. She pointed this out to my mom, who wondered aloud if it was difficult to give a home perm.

Oh no! I cringed and chewed on my straw, hoping my mom would get distracted by the two-for-one lip gloss sale. *Please lose interest in the perms!* **Please** *lose interest in the perms!*

"Wouldn't Penny look darling in curls?" Mom asked. I groaned and shook my head. *No! Is she joking? Dear God, let her be joking, and I will stop shaking the dime store's gumball machine to get extra gumballs.*

Auntie Anne, who is **usually** smart, stared at me and smiled, "Penny would look adorable in anything." That was all it took for my mom to splurge on a home perm. Three painful, smelly hours later, I stared into the bathroom mirror at my fried hair. It resembled a packet of crunchy instant noodles. When I tried running  my fingers through the tangled mess, they got stuck in the melted ends, so brushing it was out of the question. My mom had to return to the drugstore to buy me a hair pick.

I wasn't pretty before the perm. Last year I overheard my grandma refer to me as "homely." Everybody knows grandmas do nothing but brag about their grandkids. Well, everybody's but mine. I cried myself to sleep that night.

My grandma isn't the only one who thinks I'm a freak. Last week at the parent-teacher Meet & Greet, Miss Lee patted my mother's arm and said, "Gifted children are often socially awkward,

Donna, I wouldn't fret." I guess they think gifted children are also deaf; they openly discussed my lack of friends.

Miss Lee is my fourth-grade teacher. I like her, even if she did call my handwriting "a rollercoaster of don'ts." She is a bit obsessed with Care Bears and thinks we all feel the same. But she gives very little homework, so no one tells her Care Bears are babyish.

Wendy (the most popular girl in our class) said she saw Miss Lee holding hands with the school janitor, but I don't believe her. Wendy lies a lot. Mom says Wendy is starved for attention, but I think she enjoys being a liar. She's not a real friend. She's one of my soon-to-be friends; that's all I have right now.

Not to worry, this is going to be the year I stop being invisible Penny Palmer. This is going to be the year I become **popular** Penny Palmer (if my perm ever grows out).

~TWO~

I VOMIT IN FRONT OF EVERYONE

Last week, we practiced writing form letters for English class. Every time we wrote a new one, Miss Lee used mine as an example. She taped it to the chalkboard. "Notice her attention to detail, though the penmanship needs improving."

By Friday, I had four letters plastered across the chalkboard. I was slightly embarrassed by this, but at least I was no longer invisible. It also caused a stir among my classmates, who were impressed until Roger raised his hand. "Miss Lee? Are you aware all the letters on the board were written by the same author?" He smirked at me and raised his eyebrow.

At the end of the day, I noticed a letter missing from the chalkboard. Yesterday, it turned up in our home mailbox, with some revisions.

To Whom It May Concern,

I am writing because I am ~~interested~~ a Loser in learning more about your scurrying mouse cat toy.

I would like to know how ~~it runs.~~ To Stop being a Loser ~~Does it need batteries?~~ AM I Ugly?

~~Thank you for your time,~~ Sorry For My SMeLL,

Penny Palmer

Tears burning my eyes, I crumpled it up and shoved it in my pillowcase. I slammed my face into the pillow and let out an angry screech. I heard a tap on my door and turned my head to see my mom peeking in at me. I dried my eyes as she came into my room. Avoiding eye contact, I pretended to inspect my pillowcase. She smiled and said, "Penny, did you get a letter from one of your friends?"

I pulled a loose thread from the embroidery. "Sort of." *Please don't ask to see it.*

She smiled at me, "How lovely!" Parents are so clueless.

The next morning, I was determined my mood wouldn't be dampened because:

1. My home perm was behaving better,
    thanks to the Crisco I snuck out of
    the pantry and rubbed in my hair.

2. I was wearing my new sky-blue dress,
    a hand-me-down from my dad's secretary,
    Mrs. Mills.

I strolled to the front of the classroom to sharpen my pencil several times during math, so everyone could admire my new dress. I felt light on my feet as I swayed my hips from side to side while my classmates looked up at me. This was short-lived. Wendy started giggling and whispering to Becky, who glanced at me and started giggling too. My cheeks burned as their giggles turned to laughter.

Miss Lee, who believes sharing is caring, said, "Wendy, perhaps you'd like to share your anecdote with the class."

Wendy, who is starved for attention, said, "I would love to, Miss Lee." She stood up and looked at me with one nostril flared as if I stunk like broccoli. She opened her sneering lips to speak just as the recess bell rang. *Saved!* We gathered into our line, walked down the hall, and exited the building in an orderly fashion. Then we ran like crazed baboons to the playground.

I sat in the grass for most of recess because I didn't want to spoil my new dress. That was as exciting as watching Mom tweeze her eyebrows, so I moved to the tires and the monkey bars. I was about to climb up the slide when Wendy approached me. My heart began to race as she sniffed around my dress with her flared nostril. "Penny, have you been helping your dad at his grease shop?"

I jutted out my chin stubbornly. "It's not a grease shop. It's a small engine repair shop." *And I never go to his grease shop because it stinks in there.* "What are you talking about, Wendy?"

"Well, it looks like you've been working at the grease shop." She grabbed the back of my dress and pointed out a large grease stain. She smirked and folded her arms triumphantly.

I shook my head. *Boy, you really **are** starved for attention.* My cheeks grew hot as classmates gathered around us, whispering and pointing at the stain.

I eyeballed Wendy. *Seriously, it is a complete mystery how anyone can like you.* I had an idea. "Wendy, I am sorry you are so starved for attention, but at least I don't have dog poop smeared on my shoe." Wendy squealed and started scraping her foot on the ground frantically. "Wendy, why are you acting like a chicken?" I yelled. My classmates laughed, and Roger squawked and flapped his arms like a hen. I thought this would make me feel better, but it didn't. I felt worse. My stomach churned and my breakfast began coming up into my throat.

I was going to sit down, but the bell rang. I ran to the blacktop with my classmates and pushed my way into line. We barely entered the classroom when everything began to spin.

I tried taking a deep breath, but it didn't work. I raised my hand and mumbled, "Miss Lee, I'm going to be sick." The words were barely out of my mouth when I threw up...in front of everyone.

All my classmates began shrieking, pushing, and shoving. They tried to run as far away from me as possible. I'm pretty sure I heard "uncalled-for language" as my mom would say.

"*Ugh,* it smells like rotten tomatoes," Wendy claimed. She pulled her shirt over her nose and gagged.

"I think I'm going to faint," Danielle wailed. "It stinks so bad!"

Finally, Miss Lee gained control of the class, called for the janitor, and sent me to the nurse's office. I laid down on the nurse's cot and rolled up in the blankets like a hot dog. I stared at the ceiling, waiting for my mom to rescue me, and wondered if I'd ever be popular.

I stayed home for three wretched days while my mom brought me ice pops, felt my forehead, and said, "My poor baby." I've never been so bored. On day three, my mom seemed as antsy as I was. "Penny?" she gently called for the tenth time.

Honestly, don't you get tired of constant manners? I huffed and pounded my pillow into shape. "YES," I yelled.

"Penny, come down here," she practically whispered, "You know I don't approve of shouting from other rooms."

I sighed and rolled out of bed. She was not going to leave me alone. "COMING!"

When I got to the kitchen, Mom handed me her fancy stationery and said, "Wouldn't it be nice to write Mrs. Mills a thank-you note for the lovely dress?"

I shrugged, took the stationery, bunny hopped up to my room, and tossed the papers on my desk. *How annoying!*

Dear Mrs. Mills,

Thank you for the lovely

sky-blue dress. I wore it

to school, and everyone

noticed. It was a day

I'll never forget.

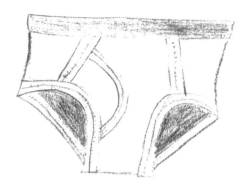

~THREE~

EVERYONE IN THEIR UNDERWEAR

Miss Lee assigned us book reports! I love writing book reports! I decided to write my report on *Anne of Green Gables.* Miss Lee gave us three weeks to complete the assignment. I can easily read that book in three days. I planned to write an A+ report, make a poster, and design some flyers to hand out to the class.

After I bought my supplies, I spent an hour making a poster of Anne (one of my best-ever pictures). Then I made a flyer listing all the reasons (there are twenty-three) why everyone should read *Anne of Green Gables.* Dad was so impressed he offered to make colored photocopies at his shop for me!

The morning of my book report I was jittery with nerves. *What if I forget everything I planned to say? Worse yet, what if I throw up*

18

again? Wendy made sure everyone remembered the last time I threw up by pinching her nose and gagging every time I walked by.

My dad tried to ease my nerves, "You know," he said, "the best way to beat nerves when you have to give a speech is to picture everyone in their underwear." He looked lost in thought as he slowly bobbed his head up and down, "No one seems intimidating when they're sitting in their underwear."

This made me laugh out loud and shoot milk through my nose. Dad smiled at me as he dabbed at the milk spray on his shirt, "You'll be fine," he promised, "just try it."

Later that morning, I sat at my table sweating and trying to calm down by imagining what kinds of underwear everyone was wearing. This only made me sweat more when the image of Miss Lee standing in front of class in her giant undies jumped into my head. I shook the image from my mind.

Miss Lee is a stickler for calling us in ABC order, and Becky's last name comes right before mine. I could feel sweat trickling down my back as I realized Becky was nearly finished. Suddenly I couldn't remember anything about my book. I began to panic. The only thing running through my brain was a picture of **me** in **my** underwear mumbling gibberish in front of the class while everyone hooted with laughter! *I'm going to throw up again!*

"Penny? Did you hear me? We are ready for your report on *Anne of Green Gables*." Miss Lee was standing right in front of my table looking less than patient. I stared up at her pursed lips and cracked make-up as the blood drained from my face. Slowly I stood up and wobbled to the front of the classroom.

I shuffled my papers around the podium and began, "Anne is a cute girl, but she hates her red hair. It is her greatest sorrow in life." I walked to the chalkboard and carefully taped my poster of Anne to it.

Some giggling began in the back of the room, and I heard Wendy loudly whisper, "I bet Penny's perm is **her** greatest sorrow." I glared at Wendy and pictured her shrinking down into a chirping cricket. I resisted the urge to squish the cricket with my shoe and kept going.

"Anne is really smart, and she works hard in school. Even though she is an orphan, people love her." I then passed around my colorful flyers and paused to give everyone time to read them.

More giggling from the back, and this time Roger whispered something inaudible which made half of the class erupt into laughter. Miss Lee clapped her hands and stood up, "Class, let us remember to show our respect to everyone by quietly listening to their reports." Roger showed his respect by quietly using my flyer to make a paper airplane. It whizzed past my head, and I ducked as several more flyers sailed by.

Miss Lee was irate. "That is enough!" She marched up to the chalkboard and wrote the word "Respect" in large letters. The room grew perfectly still as she continued, "Since you are all ignorant of the meaning of this word, you will write a two-page report on its definition. Due tomorrow." She smacked the chalk down, and I swallowed a giant lump in my throat. *Great. Now everyone will hate me even more!*

I cut short my disaster of a report, as my eyes brimmed with tears. "I think everyone should read *Anne of Green Gables* because it is a fun book, and we are all a bit like Anne," I mumbled, ripping my poster off the chalkboard.

Roger stuck his leg out into the aisle, trying to trip me, as I hurried back to my seat. "Is that poster supposed to be a person, Penny," he sneered, "because it looks like a potato."

Graceful as a little goat, I hopped over Roger's leg and turned around to face him. I took a deep breath, "Roger, you look **ridiculous** sitting there in your Scooby-Doo underwear!"

~FOUR~

A BASKETBALL AND A SLEEPOVER

Tuesdays we have gym class. Normally, I love it, but we are in the middle of a basketball unit, and I do not like basketball **at all**. The ball is huge and impossible to hold. Also, a few of the girls are getting weirdly aggressive about this game. Coach (what everyone calls our gym teacher) played basketball at some big college, so he is enthusiastic about this unit. His enthusiasm has infected everyone except for me.

It was, unfortunately, Tuesday, and as soon as I stepped onto the gym floor, Wendy whipped the ball at me. I winced as it slapped against the palms of my hands. *You would, wouldn't you? Aggressive Weirdo!* I dribbled it five clumsy steps. Heart racing, I glanced over the gym floor, looking for an open teammate. *Nothing!*

It was then I discovered Coach's disdain for me as I heard him say, "Take it from her if she's going to stand there!" Priscilla lunged at me and grabbed the ball from my limp grip. Grunting, she launched it toward the hoop. We watched as it bounced off the rim and shot back down…right onto my nose.

*"**Oww**!" My face is exploding! I'm bleeding! Oh my goodness, that's a lot of blood! Help! Someone, help me! Wait, is anyone hearing me? No, I don't think I'm speaking. My mouth isn't working. Help! Maybe if I wave my arms…*

"Gross! Look at Penny!" Priscilla stood over me as I laid on the floor, marveling at how short my life was. *I didn't even make it to double digits…*

"Eww…disgusting!" Wendy chimed in with one of her never helpful comments.

"Whoa! Look at Penny's face! That's messed up."

Thank you, Roger, for pointing out the obvious.

Roger stuck his greasy face next to mine; then everything went black.

I opened my eyes to the nurse leaning over me as I laid, again, on her cot. It took everything in me not to slap her as she stuffed scraggly

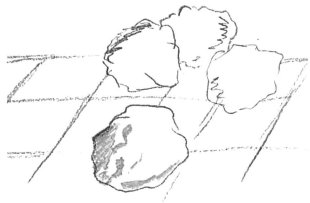

23

cotton ball pieces up my nose to stop the bleeding. Basketball is **worse** than book reports.

I thought the whole book report thing and the basketball incident had torpedoed my chance to be popular, so I was elated when Wendy invited me to a sleepover at her house! Well, technically her mom invited **all** the girls in our class, but still! Everyone was excitedly talking about the sleepover. I was nervous because this was my first sleepover, but if things went well, maybe it would be the beginning of my rise to popularity.

During free time, I made a list of what to bring and, more importantly, what to leave home. I gave a lot of thought to my *Care Bears* sleeping bag before putting it in the "Leave Home" column. Its inside is soft as feathers, and I love the lavender smell from my cedar chest. But the sleeping bag looks babyish, and that's the last thing I need, being called a baby. I moved my pen to the "Bring With" column and wrote, "Dad's army blanket." It smells like cat pee and is annoyingly scratchy, but I can't take any unnecessary risks.

I debated which pajamas to bring. My white cotton nightgown is pretty, but I'm not sure if nightgowns are proper sleepover attire. The other option is my bright yellow ducky pajamas (which are kind of babyish, but they have a neat-looking hood with a beak), which I think is cool.

A definite on my "Bring With" column was my friendship bracelets. I made seven bracelets, and this was the perfect opportunity to give them away!

I was almost packed for the sleepover when my mom came into my room. "Penny, darling, what is on your cheek?"

"Nothing, Mom." *Something very itchy.*

"Well, it's something. Let me see." My mom cupped my face in her hands. "I don't like the looks of this," she mumbled.

I squirmed and pushed her hands away. *I wouldn't touch it. They are spreading.* "It's nothing, Mom. I need to get ready for Wendy's."

Her eyes grew wide. "Darling, that isn't nothing, and there's another one on your neck!"

And about twenty on my belly.

Mom frowned as she stared at more spots on my body. "Penny, I think I better take you to see Sue." Sue is my mom's best friend. She is a doctor at the clinic in town and is, unfortunately, always willing to see me.

I shook my head and backed away. "Please, Mom, I feel fine, just a little itchy." *Rip-off-my-flesh kind of itchy.* "I don't want to be late for the sleepover." *Because this may be my only invitation ever.*

"It will only take a few minutes at the clinic, and we'll go straight to Wendy's from there. Best to be safe, Darling." She softly patted my cheek and smiled at me.

I have the plague! Well, I might as well have. As usual, Sue was no help at all. Sternly, she looked me in the eyes and said I was to "go straight home." There was no sleepover and no rise to popularity for me.

When I got home, I ran to my room, dumped my bracelets in my bottom dresser drawer, flopped onto my bed, and cried. I wriggled toward my pillow and rubbed my cheek against the blanket. This made my spots itch more, and I squirmed around trying to get comfortable. But the more I squirmed, the worse I itched! This was the worst thing that could have happened! I wrapped myself in Dad's army blanket and gagged at the smell of cat pee.

There was a soft tap on my door, then Mom poked her head in the room. "Penny, darling," she whispered.

I clutched the blanket tighter and groaned. *No! Please go away!*

She walked over, sat on the bed, and rubbed my back. "Daddy and I thought we could have a sleepover right here at home, in the living room. We'll watch movies and order pizza and stay up late, whatever you want."

I knew my parents were trying to make it better, but nothing could make it better. "Maybe another time, Mom. I want to go to sleep now." *And claw at my rash.*

Even though I wanted to be alone, I didn't want her to leave. I think she knew it, because she continued rubbing my back and letting me cry.

~FIVE~

ALL I WANT FOR CHRISTMAS

Daddy-daughter date, that's what my mom calls it. I know it is a ruse to get me out of the house so my mom can shop and wrap Christmas presents—that is fine with me. I circled seventeen things in the Sears catalog and dropped not-so-subtle hints. One thing my heart is longing for is an olive-green, suede leather jacket. I know they are impossible to find in my size, but I am willing to wear a too-big jacket for a couple of years, if it is suede and olive-green.

27

Dad took me to supper at Two Scoop Scoopies. They have the best burgers in town and chocolate peanut butter fudge ice cream. I planned to skimp on my dinner, so I would have room for both scoops.

At the restaurant, my dad talked about his latest engine projects. I smiled and acted interested, but my mind wandered to the jacket in the Sears catalog. *I wonder if Mom is purchasing it at this very moment.* I tried to concentrate on what my dad was saying, but kept fidgeting with the silverware as I pictured my mom's hand sliding her tidy pile of dollar bills across the Sears sales counter…the smiling saleslady handing over an olive-green, suede leather…

My dad stared at me. "Penny Pie? Did you hear me?" I realized I had no idea what he said.

I jumped a bit, knocking over my water glass. "Umm, yes, it needed spark plugs." *As good a guess as any.*

"No," my dad laughed as he mopped up the spill with his napkin. "I asked what you want Santa to bring you."

I quickly glanced around to make sure none of my classmates were nearby. Santa Claus was **so** babyish. "Oh, honestly, Daddy. You know I don't believe in Santa."

My dad smiled and winked. "Well, what do you want the elves to bring?"

I rolled my eyes and ignored the question. "Daddy, were you popular when you were my age?"

"Not particularly, no. Why do you ask?" He leaned his head a bit and looked softly at me.

"Oh, wondering what you were like as a boy is all."

My dad eyed me curiously. He watched the soda bubbles fizzle in his glass before replying. "I was…"

"Two burgers," the waitress interrupted. "Watch the plates," she cooed, "they're a bit hot."

Dad and I reached for the ketchup bottle at the same time, but he was faster. He squeezed some on my burger and then on his. The ketchup bottle made a loud belching sound. We both laughed because it was funny, and because my mom wasn't with.

He smiled and wound the straw wrapper between his fingers thoughtfully. "Penny," he asked slowly, "how is fourth grade working out for you?"

One big nightmare after another. I looked at him for a few seconds then shrugged, "Okay, I guess."

Dad nodded his head slowly and looked at me with concern. He wasn't fooled, but he was nice enough to pretend. "Were you able to give away all those friendship bracelets you made?"

"Well, not all of them," I lied.

It was quiet, except for the sound of our chewing. Then my dad said, "I think your hair is pretty tonight."

I snorted and bit into my burger. Dad is terrible at lying. "I hate my home perm."

"I know you do, but it does look pretty tonight. It's shiny." He winked.

Maybe I better lay off the Crisco for a while. I pulled on a curl and smoothed the frizz. "Thanks, Daddy. I guess it's starting to grow out a bit."

My dad smiled and reached his hand across the table. I put my hand in his. There was something about my small hand inside his big hand that made me believe I was pretty.

He winked at me. "All full, Penny Pie?"

I shook my head, "Not too full for ice cream."

~Six~

THE BEST CHRISTMAS EVER

Miss Lee assigned the Christmas pageant roles on Monday. Normally, I cross my fingers and hope for a non-part in the choir, but this year I was desperate to be Mary. Surely having the lead role in the school play would boost my popularity. All the girls, except Becky, wanted the part, so Miss Lee decided to have try-outs.

We each did a dramatic reading of a poem in front of the class. I didn't see how it related to the role of Mary, but I cooperated because I needed the part.

We traipsed to the library and made our poem selections. Most of the girls picked a Shell Silverstein piece. I chose "Sonnet 43" by Elizabeth Barrett Browning. It is my favorite poem, and I wanted to stand out.

I barely listened as the rest of the girls read. No one (in my opinion) was as good as me. At least Miss Lee didn't say, "What an ambitious poem selection," to the other readers. The only girl who came close was Wendy, because, well, Wendy is great at everything. *How annoying.*

Miss Lee stood up and smiled at our group. "Thank you, ladies, for trying out. You were all wonderful, but please remember there's only one Mary." Several girls stared at Wendy, who flipped her hair as if knowing she'd be Mary. *Won't you be surprised!*

Instead, I was the one surprised when ten minutes later Miss Lee handed me a slip of paper with the words "Heavenly Host Angel #2" printed on it.

My heart lurched and sank into my stomach. I could tell by Wendy's high-pitched squeal who got the Mary part. I knew I should congratulate her,

but I decided to take the bathroom pass and go for a walk instead.

After two weeks of practice, it was finally the night of the pageant. My mom fussed for almost an hour over my angel costume, trying to make it fit better. It is impossible to make a raggedy old sheet look good, and she finally gave up and moved on to my hair.

Usually it resembles a dandelion, but miraculously it relaxed enough to get a brush through it. She brushed and sprayed it, then put it in a bun using about a hundred bobby pins. Mom stepped back, looked at my hair, and shook her head. "It looks so pretty down. Let's not bother with a bun." That really meant, "It looks awful no matter what."

Mom pursed her lips as she ran her fingers through my hair. "Penny, darling, I think you better shampoo more often. Your hair feels greasy." *Not for long, I used the last of the Crisco last night.*

Miss Lee made all the angels a tinsel crown to wear, along with tinsel wings. Mom twisted and reshaped mine before pinning them onto my sheet. "There. Much more elegant," she tilted her head and stared at me a moment. After one more tweak of my wings, she seemed satisfied with my appearance. She made me rehearse my one little line on the way to school. I was still fuming a bit over not being Mary and couldn't muster much enthusiasm for my angel part.

At school, I peeked out from behind the stage curtain. I scanned the audience until I found my parents in the second row looking proud and calm. I stood with the other heavenly host, waiting our turn to say our one line in perfect unison. I knew the entire play by heart, and my mind kept wandering to page seventy-three in the Sears catalog.

Finally, the narrator gave us our cue, "Suddenly a great company of the heavenly host appeared with the angel, praising God and saying..."

We glided out on stage and in not quite perfect unison, but with perfect heart, all the Mary-rejects said, "Glory to God in the highest heaven, and on earth peace to those on whom his favor rests."

I drifted off for the rest of the play, which was essentially Wendy filling up her hungry void. I squinted and looked out at the sea of faces. Most were familiar because I have always lived here, and my school is small. As I looked from face to face, I found myself wondering about God's favor, wondering if it rests on me.

On Christmas morning, I ran downstairs and dumped my stocking onto the floor, watching its contents spill out and roll around. Mom always lets me ransack my stocking before breakfast, but the wrapped gifts are forbidden until after we eat.

As always, the stocking was filled with all the things I love: neon scrunchies, perfume in a heart-shaped bottle, fuzzy purple socks, chocolate-flavored Chapstick, pear-scented hand lotion, a box of stationery (my mom and her thank-you notes), the Bee Gees' latest cassette tape, and a pen shaped like a tube of lipstick.

Dad winked at me as I walked into the kitchen. "Merry Christmas, Penny!" Whistling Christmas carols, he dropped a dot of water on the griddle. I watched, mesmerized, as it bubbled and danced in the grease. I took my place at the table and waited impatiently for him to serve his Santa shaped pancakes.

After several minutes, and many off-key tunes, he set a giant plate of misshapen Santa cakes in front of me. *Finally!* I stuffed my pancakes into my mouth as fast as I could, choking a little. Syrup dribbled down my chin and onto my mom's Christmas tablecloth. I burped, wiped at the syrup, coughed a hunk of pancake out of my throat where it had lodged, and shoved more pancakes in. My mom, overcome with Christmas spirit, cleared her throat and took a small bite, ignoring my lack of table manners.

I helped my mom clean up the kitchen (only because she made me). Then we sat down in the living room to open our presents.

My dad got one boring tool after another. My mom and I *oohed* and *ahhed* over each one. He is never surprised by his gifts because every year we buy straight from his list called "Tools I Need." This year was no exception, but he was pleased.

I always make my mom's gift. She says homemade is the best kind, and I believe she means it. I continued this tradition with a

35

picture frame made from sea glass, collected on our last vacation to Florida. Inside the frame, the picture showed the three of us smiling brightly as we played on the beach. My mom fondly traced her finger around the sea glass, and I could see a tear in the corner of her eye. "It's perfect, Penny. I couldn't love it more." She gave me a hug and said she knew just where to hang it.

I squirmed and tried to hide a smile as Dad handed my mom a long, slender envelope. I knew what he got for her. He went a little crazy and used half his paycheck to buy her a day at the beauty salon, something she had wanted since Auntie Anne splurged on one for herself.

"A single gal must stay in the game," she told my mom when she finished her day of beauty. I didn't say anything, but she looked exactly the same.

My mom opened the envelope containing the gift certificate for the salon and said, "Oh, Al! How did you know? I can't believe you did this! It must have cost a fortune." I rolled my eyes and looked away as my mom planted a big kiss on Dad's lips. I hate it when they kiss in front of me.

I cleared my throat. "Ahem, you're forgetting someone, like...me!"

Dad smiled and ruffled my hair. "We could never forget you, Penny Pie. You are right though. It's your turn."

I grabbed the smallest box first. Inside was an assortment of beads, clasps, and string of varying colors—more friendship bracelets. *Wow, you are really clueless. You have no idea I don't have any friends, not one.* "Thank you! These are perfect! I will be the coolest girl in school with these. Everyone will be begging for one." I stopped when I realized I was babbling.

I moved on to the middle-size box and gave it a gentle shake. It was too small for the olive-colored jacket I desperately wanted—probably clothes, another disappointment. I stared at the bright wrapping paper, wishing the jacket into the box. Mom knew how much I wanted the jacket. It just had to be there!

Fingers trembling, I pulled at the stubborn tape, ripped the lid off the box, and found two new pairs of stirrup pants. One pair was purple and one was red with black stripes around the ankles, perfect for under my dresses, but not what I truly wanted.

One last box sat under the tree, beautifully wrapped with shiny silver paper and a gold bow. I gently untied the bow and slowly peeled back the paper. Inside was another clothes box, but this one was labeled "Sears." I could hardly breathe from anticipation. *What if it's a new dress for school? How will I fake excitement?* I carefully opened the box and pulled back the tissue paper. *Please be the jacket. Please be the jacket.*

And there it was, my olive-green, suede leather jacket. My mouth turned dry, and I felt a lump form in my throat. I couldn't believe it was truly mine. I traced my finger on the soft suede. I wanted to shout, *My beautiful jacket!* Suddenly tears were running down my cheeks, and a sob escaped my tight throat.

"Darling?" My mom touched my shoulder, "Is it the one you wanted?" she asked nervously.

I stared at her dumbly for a couple seconds, and then I leaped at the couch, where they sat holding hands, and hugged them both as tight as I could.

I know it is just a jacket, there are more important things in life, but getting this jacket made me believe God's favor **does** rest on me.

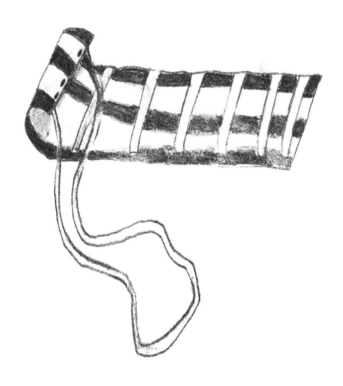

~SEVEN~

ANOTHER INVITATION!

On our first day back after Christmas vacation, I proudly strolled into school wearing my beautiful jacket. I was prepared for the stir it would cause. *Why, yes, this **is** suede. I know it's tempting, but please stop touching the jacket...*

"Is that your mom's jacket, Penny?" Leave it to Wendy to point out the size.

"No. I wanted one big enough to fit me more than one season," I lied.

Wendy *hmphed* and flipped her hair back. "Well, it will last you **many** seasons."

My cheeks flushed, and I could feel my shoulders slump down inside my too-big jacket. "I hope it does. My parents spent a lot of money on it." *Didn't you get enough attention starring in the Christmas pageant?*

Wendy shrugged and stared at me. "Oh. Well, it's a pretty color."

Was that a compliment? I felt my shoulders straighten. "Thank you. I think so too."

"Anyway, I wanted to give you this. It's an invitation to my sledding party this weekend." She handed me a neon pink envelope. Shocked, I stared at the envelope, my mouth hanging open. I was too stunned to speak; I stood there, stupidly. She scrunched her eyebrows and stared at me. "You have to bring your own sled."

After a beat, I heard my wobbly voice saying, "Okay, I will. Thanks, Wendy." *YES! YES! YES!*

On the day of the party, I didn't pack my friendship bracelets, mainly because there was nowhere to keep them. I stood in our kitchen, glancing at the clock, and trying not to roll my eyes. The only way Mom agreed I could go to Wendy's party was if I agreed to some "ground rules." So there I stood, listening to my mother's "do's and don'ts" list for what seemed like the hundredth time.

"And, Darling, be sure to check the bottom of the hill each time before going down. Remember, Auntie Anne broke her arm sledding down Grandpa's hill."

I sighed and stared at the wallpaper pattern. *For pity's sake, that was twenty years ago, and there was a barn in the way!* The familiar *whirring* sound of Dad starting the car interrupted my thoughts. In just minutes, I'd be on my way to Wendy's party and popularity.

"Penny, did you hear me?" My mom raised her eyebrows waiting for a response.

"Oh…umm…yes, Auntie Anne's arm." *Blah, blah, blah.*

Mom looked irritated and tired. "No, Darling, I asked if you're sure you'll be warm enough in that jacket."

I gritted my teeth and managed a fake smile. "Yes, it's surprisingly warm." It was "surprisingly" because the jacket isn't warm at all, but I'd rather turn into a walking popsicle than wear anything else.

"My mother frowned and cupped my face in her hands. "Are you okay, Penny? If you're not feeling well…"

I jerked away from Mom, panicked. There was no way I'd miss Wendy's party **again**. "I'm fine! I'm just getting hot with this jacket on," I insisted as I pulled at the collar. As if on cue, Dad honked the car horn. "I'll be fine," I promised, planting a kiss on her face before running out the door.

41

My dad beamed at me as I tossed my sled into the car. "Well, Penny Pie, ready to show the world what you're made of?"

I smiled brightly. "Oh, Daddy, it's just sledding." *And yes, that's **exactly** what I'm ready to do!*

My dad tousled the pompom on my hat, then we drove in silence to the big hill at the park across town. Butterflies tap-danced in my stomach as I watched my classmates gathering at the bottom of the hill. *There's no need for nerves*, I told myself. I briefly pictured everyone sledding in their underwear, but this made me feel even colder inside my thin jacket.

I jumped out of the car as soon as we parked and waved to my dad, without even pausing to hear what he was saying. "DON'T PICK ME UP BEFORE THREE!" I shouted, running toward my soon-to-be friends.

After two hours of sledding and zero moments of me humiliating myself, we all stood together at the bottom of the hill. I was dusting snow from my head when I heard Wendy say, "I like your pompom hat." I looked around to see who she was talking to. She meant me.

"Thanks, Wendy." I cooly replied, trying to sound less excited than I felt. She lost interest in my hat and walked over to Becky. They grabbed their sleds and started the climb up the big hill.

I hadn't spoken to Roger since the book report incident, but Wendy's compliment gave me courage. I smiled at him and said, "Hello, Roger," as indifferently as I could manage.

"Hey, Penny," he mumbled. Roger is such a dweeb.

Danielle asked if I wanted to race down the hill. We grabbed our sleds and ran up the hill, laughing and panting. At the top, we lined up, and Danielle said, "Ready, set, go!" I pushed off and felt the cold air slapping my face. I could hardly breathe as I sucked in the icy wind. Before we reached the bottom (I was winning), our sleds collided, and we went sailing out of them, landing in a snowbank. We laughed so hard we barely heard Wendy's mom calling everyone to the warming shelter for hot chocolates.

When everyone was huddled in the shelter, Wendy's mom began handing out steaming cups of hot cocoa. She obviously miscounted because everyone had a cup but me. I stared at the snow melting off my boots, hoping no one would notice this embarrassing oversight.

Wendy, who notices everything, cleared her throat, "Mom, Penny doesn't have one."

Her mom *tsked* and tapped a flawlessly painted fingernail against her teeth. "Oh dear, I must have counted wrong."

*Counting to **twelve** can be difficult…*

"Penny, are you terribly thirsty, or can you do without?"

No one drinks hot chocolate for thirst, lady! "I'm fine, Mrs. Simms, not too thirsty." I felt my windburned cheeks getting redder.

"I could run back to the cafe for more cups," she suggested. "Would anyone else like a second hot chocolate?"

***Second** hot chocolate? How about my **first** cup?*

My classmates remained silent; Mrs. Simms assumed no one wanted a **second** cup. Everyone was gawking as if I were a strange bug, creepy, but still interesting. Finally, Roger shrugged and said, "Penny can have mine. I don't like hot chocolate much anyway."

Liar. Everyone likes hot chocolate. I couldn't decide if I should trust him, but everyone was waiting for my response. "Thanks, Roger, that's really nice of you," I muttered stiffly. Roger and I reached out our hands at the same moment, and we collided. Before I could jump back, hot chocolate splashed onto my beautiful, olive-green, suede leather jacket. There was a moment of stunned silence as my classmates watched the liquid drip off my sleeve. Becky giggled nervously, and soon everyone was laughing at my ruined jacket.

44

Barely able to see, I choked out a "thank you" to Mrs. Simms and plunged through the group of kids. The icy wind whipped my face as I ran out of the shelter and up the big hill. Before my tears spilled from my eyes, I saw my blurry dad waving from across the parking lot. I sprinted the last few yards and threw myself into his arms.

~EIGHT~

A VALENTINE...FOR ME?

Valentine's Day is my favorite holiday. Miss Lee must like it too because the Friday before Valentine's, she asked everyone to decorate a small cardboard mailbox for "all the cards our friends will want to give us." She set up a special table in front of the classroom for us to "proudly display our boxes as we watch them fill up." True to form, she plastered Tenderheart Bear's picture behind the table and handed each of us a dirty old shoebox to decorate. All were missing

46

their lids, and some only had three sides, but I supposed they would look better after we decorated them.

I love making cards. When we finished decorating our valentine mailboxes, I skipped home and spent the entire weekend making cards for everyone in my class, including Miss Lee.

"Mom!" I yelled down the stairs.

I heard a *thunk*, and then my mom muttering, "Good grief." A few seconds later she pitter-pattered up the stairs and into my room. "Penny, please come find me when you want to talk instead of yelling all the time." She folded her arms across her chest. "What is it you need?"

"We have to make cards for school, and I was wondering if you would help me make cloth envelopes." I smiled innocently at her and gave her my pleading eyes. Cloth envelopes would not be an easy task since my mom barely knew how to thread the sewing machine. My pleading eyes worked, though, and she agreed to help.

We worked on the cards first. We cut and pasted and wrote friendship poems. We even used cookie cutters for tracing and left-over sprinkles for decorations. "How do you like this one?" I held up a card with two gingerbread people holding a heart between them. It had tiny snowflake candies glued all over it.

Mom smiled and gently took the card, "Penny, I think you are a creative wonder." She patted my cheek and handed me more sprinkles.

It took us two hours to make all the envelopes, but they looked amazing. I kept one for myself, tucking it safely in my dresser drawer next to my friendship bracelets.

On Monday, I proudly brought my valentines to school and conspicuously stuffed them in everyone's boxes. *Look at my beautiful cards! Don't you want to give me one in return?* I didn't see a mailbox for Miss Lee, so I put hers in my math folder for safe-keeping.

Three days later, I sat in my seat during math class, stewing about the valentine boxes. Mine sat empty, not one card in it. I wrote in my notebook, pressing down until the pencil lead broke.

Zero cards + Zero cards = 1 loser

And that loser is me. My gaze wandered from box to box, stopping on a brightly decorated, bulging one. It was Wendy's, of course. *How many valentines are in there?* I began counting. *Thirteen. Yes, I'm sure I see thirteen. There are only twelve of us in class. Did Miss Lee give Wendy a valentine? And did Wendy give one to herself? It doesn't add up.*

"Penny?" Miss Lee was standing over my table.

I covered my scribbles with my hand. "Yes, Miss Lee?"

Miss Lee raised her eyebrows impatiently. "I hope it is a math problem causing you such distraction."

*It certainly **is** a math problem.* "Yes, Miss Lee, I'm working one out in my head." *Twelve students plus one teacher equals a full box of valentines.*

I finished all the math problems and brought them up to Miss Lee's desk for her to check. *Maybe I can subtly find out if she gave Wendy a valentine.*

My muscles relaxed as Ms. Lee marked my paper with a red checkmark. "Excellent. All correct as usual, Penny. Good work." She handed me my math sheet and nodded for me to take my seat.

I paused for a moment trying to decide what to say. "Thanks, Miss Lee...I was wondering if you were planning to decorate a valentine mailbox too." *Did you, or did you not, give Wendy a valentine?*

Ms. Lee smiled and leaned back in her chair. "How nice of you to think of me. Yes, I have one at home I will bring in."

I blushed and scuffed my shoe on the floor. "Okay, because some of us made you a card." *And you obviously made **some** of us a card as well.*

She smiled patiently. "That's very sweet, Penny. You may sit back down and work on your extra credit until the others finish."

I clumped back to my seat and scribbled in my notebook. *And **you** may put a valentine in **my** mailbox seeing as **you** started this whole valentine disaster.*

49

The day of our valentine party arrived. I put on my ruffly pink dress and squeezed my feet into my old red cowboy boots. I was determined to enjoy the party. I wasn't going to care if my mailbox held only two cards, like it did at 2:45 yesterday afternoon. I wasn't going to care if Wendy's too-full mailbox burst apart. *I hope it explodes.* I wasn't even going to care if Roger said my perm looked like Cupid's arrows sprouting from my head, which he did yesterday and the day before.

I bunny-hopped down the stairs two at a time and twirled into the kitchen, watching my dress fan out.

Dad smiled and whistled. "Wowee, Penny Pie, you are a sight for this old man's eyes!"

I grinned at him. "Daddy, thirty-five isn't **that** old."

My dad winked at me. "Does that mean you'll be my valentine?"

"Hey! What about Mom?" I gave him my best horrified expression.

He tilted his head and scrunched his nose, "I don't know. She's getting kind of old; don't you think?"

"Daddy!"

My dad laughed and tossed me an orange. He picked up the newspaper and buried his head in it. I plunked the orange back into the fruit bowl and grabbed a banana instead. I opened the pantry and pulled out the Grape Nuts. After I loaded them up with sugar and milk, I set them on the counter to soak and twirled over to the stool next to my dad. It was cold, but the sun was pouring in the kitchen window. I slid my stool over, enjoying the warmth of the sunbeam. I looked around and realized Mom was nowhere to be seen. "Daddy, what happened to Mom?" I demanded, eyeing him curiously as I peeled my banana.

"She's off to her day of beauty at the salon." Dad peeked over the top of the newspaper, his eyes twinkling. "Do you think we'll recognize her when she gets home? Because I'm terrified we may not."

I giggled and swatted at his newspaper. "Oh, Daddy, you're being silly. She'll probably look exactly the same."

"Too true, Penny Pie, too true." He shook his head mournfully and went back to reading his paper.

My Grape Nuts were the perfect amount of soggy. I ate as slowly as I could, slurping the sugary milk from the bottom of the bowl. I can get away with this when it is just me and my dad.

I wiped my lips with the back of my hand and put the bowl in the sink. "I better go, Daddy," I said, kissing his cheek, "we have a valentine party today." The minute the words were out of my mouth, I felt like pinching myself. *Now he'll ask me about it when I get home, and I'll have to tell him what a loser his daughter is.*

Later that day, I sat at Friend Bear table, staring at my valentine mailbox, which resembled a sad deserted toy store. I was trying not to compare it to everyone else's. *At least there are a few more cards than yesterday. That brings my total to five.*

Miss Lee brought in her four-sided valentine mailbox (with lid) this morning, and it was already as full as Wendy's. *I don't care*, I reminded myself. I looked around the table at my fellow Friend Bears and wondered why fourth grade was easier for them. *Why is my mailbox the emptiest?*

Miss Lee gave us one last opportunity to write valentine cards for our friends. I doodled in my notebook. I had already made everyone a card, and I didn't **have** any friends. Miss Lee stood up and cleared her throat. "Time's up. Deliver the last of your cards and return to your seats, please." I remembered Miss Lee's card still stuffed in my math folder and pulled it out. I walked up to the mailboxes and gently placed it inside her felt-covered box. I returned to my seat and slumped in my chair, watching as classmates milled around the boxes. I took a deep breath and held it. *I don't care. Whatever happens, I don't care.*

Ms. Lee smiled and clapped her hands for attention. "Alright class, settle down. We will begin our party as soon as Roger returns from the restroom. In the meantime, I'm going to read you the true story of St. Valentine."

My mind wandered. For a moment, I was relaxing with Mom at the salon, then I was helping Dad at his grease shop. What I really wanted was to be in my cozy ducky pajamas, curled up under my blankets.

Miss Lee finished her story just as Roger returned from his walk. He never goes to the restroom. I know this because I use the girls' bathroom pass to take walks, and sometimes we pass each other in the hall. We have an unspoken pact never to tattle on each other.

Miss Lee closed the book and laid it on her desk. "And now boys and girls, I need you to quietly take your boxes back to your table…" No one heard any more because everyone was pushing and reaching and grabbing for their boxes. With a *whoop,* Roger hurdled his chair and was at the front of the room in two strides. My feet were like lead as I slowly made my way to my box.

To my surprise, my mailbox had **seven** cards in it, two of them buried on the bottom. I felt a ray of hope. *Maybe people* ***do*** *like me. I only* ***imagined*** *I'm friendless. Maybe I'm becoming* ***popular****!*

I took all seven cards out of my mailbox and carefully set them on the table in front of me. My hands shook as I slowly tore open the first envelope. Inside was a pretty pink card with a bear holding a heart. At least, I thought it was a bear. *Whoever drew this isn't artistic, but it doesn't matter. The important thing is someone made this card especially for me.* I opened the card to see what was written inside.

> Penny, you are bear-y ugly.
> Ha-ha. Love, Friend Bear

My stomach lurched. I felt the familiar burn in my cheeks. *I don't care. It's only one card. It's probably from Roger. He thinks he's so clever. Forget our pact. I'm tattling next time he wanders the hall.*

I opened my second envelope. The card was flowered with a lace doily glued to the front. It was sloppy, and they clearly did not follow the dot-dot-not-a-lot glue rule. I shrugged. *Oh well, it's still a card, and it's still for me.* I carefully opened it.

Penny's puffy perm is perfectly...

A lump formed in my throat, and I could feel a snot drip sliding down my lip. I quickly closed the card before anyone could see. I stuffed all the valentines back into my dirty shoebox, not even looking at the rest.

I plastered a fake smile on my face and acted happy throughout the party. I laughed during our game of pin the hearts on Cupid's arrow. I skipped during musical chairs. I smiled the rest of the entire school day because ***I DON'T CARE!***

That evening I laid on my bed, comfortable in my ducky pajamas, the hood with the cool duck beak pulled down over my eyes. I stared at the friendship bracelets on my blankets, the brightly-colored strings as tangled as my thoughts.

The more I stared at those bracelets, the more I thought about the hateful Valentine's Day cards, and the more my stomach knotted in anger. *How can someone like Wendy act so mean and have all the friends? I've been nice, haven't I? I don't have one, not one friend.* A giant swoop of my arm and the bracelets went sailing off the bed. "Not like I need those anyway," I sniffed.

"Penny Pie, can I come in," my dad asked, tapping on my bedroom door.

I was in no mood for questions, and I knew there would be several if my dad saw my tearstained cheeks and puffy eyes. I pulled the hood further over my face and mumbled, "Come in."

Dad stepped over a pile of clothes on the floor and set a large bag on my bed. I glanced at it, then busied myself picking up the fallen bracelets. "How was the party, Penny Pie?"

"Pretty good." I kept my face down, hoping my hood covered my eyes.

"Are you making more bracelets?" He picked one up and twirled it around his fingers.

"No, fixing the leftovers." *Go, just go,* I pleaded silently.

Instead, he sat on the bed and pushed the bag toward me. "Happy Valentine's Day, Penny Pie."

Now I was curious. "Umm…thanks. What's that?"

He nudged me. "Open it and see."

I didn't want to disappoint my dad. I reached into the bag and lifted out my olive-green, suede leather jacket. "Daddy! How did you do it? I thought it was ruined!"

Dad kissed the top of my head. "Dry cleaning works wonders, Penny Pie."

It was perfectly clean, without a trace of hot chocolate on it. I hugged it to my body and buried my face in it. *I love the smell of suede.* "Thank you, Daddy! Thank you so much!" I leaned my whole body into him and let out a long, wobbly breath.

For the first time that day, I **didn't** care. I fell asleep snuggled under the best present ever.

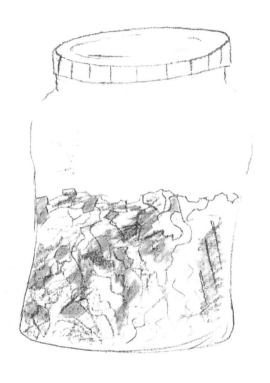

~NINE~

I'M A TRENDSETTER!

Wendy and some of the girls have a club that meets at recess. They call themselves The Kitty Cats and have a secret *meow* signal they use to show they belong. They meet at the top of the tornado slide, the only spot on the playground out of the wind.

I do **not** like the wind or the cold weather. It makes my nose burn and my eyes water, causing my eyelashes to freeze. I think The

Kitty Cats is a silly club with a stupid name and a dumb secret signal, but I want to become a member when the wind gusts snow into my eyes, and my eyelashes frost over. The club sounds absurd, but the shelter of the tornado slide sounds like heaven.

I tried casually mentioning my becoming a member of The Kitty Cats to Wendy, but she hissed at me. I asked Becky about joining. She asked if I knew the secret signal. I gave my best cat imitation, but it was no use. I sounded like my grandma's cat, Nimble, when she backed over his tail with her car.

Becky said she wished she could help me, but there was no way I could be part of The Kitty Cats without knowing the secret signal. *How ridiculous! Obviously, no one knows the signal **before** becoming a Kitty Cat.* I gave up on recess altogether and discovered the teachers' restroom was far more heavenly than the top of the tornado slide. There is a cozy nook with the loveliest pink vanity. The top drawer has little soaps shaped like seashells and a box of perfumed cloths. It is always clean and smells like potpourri.

One day, while enjoying my hideout, I wiped those perfumed cloths on my wrists. I took a big whiff. *Mmm, flowers.* I rubbed them on my ankles too. I stared in the mirror and made a fish face at my reflection. My perm was wearing off, but my hair still resembled broken bedsprings. I took a brush from the middle drawer and brushed my hair 100 strokes. I smiled as I turned my head from side to side. *Better. I wonder what else they have in the drawers.*

As I reached for the bottom drawer, I heard the bathroom door swoosh open. High heels were clicking toward me. I shoved the drawer shut and ducked into a stall to hide. I crouched on the toilet seat with my feet tucked up under me, trying to be silent. The clicking heels came closer and

stopped in the stall next to me. I waited while High Heels took her time.

My left foot started to go numb. I tried silently rubbing life back into it, but I lost my balance and bonked into the toilet paper, which broke free and rolled under my stall into hers. Silence. Then an uncomfortable cough followed by a kick of a heel, and my toilet paper came rolling back. I didn't dare pick it up until High Heels left. Finally, she flushed, and after a ridiculous amount of handwashing, she clicked out into the hall.

I reseated myself at the vanity and smeared on deodorant samples from the bottom drawer, to see what they were like. They smelled nice, like lilacs, but left weird white streaks on my dress. I decided to stick with perfumed cloths in the future. I rummaged around a bit more but only found embarrassing lady items. Students are forbidden in here, so I made up for my misdeed by tidying the vanity and wiping down the sink and mirror before I left.

I can't believe it! I'm a trendsetter! This is a turning point in my popularity, I am sure of it. It began on Friday when I found my mom's old paper punch in the garbage. After washing off the coffee grounds, I brought it to my dad. "Could you fix this, Daddy?"

He laughed as he took the punch and turned it over in his hands. "No job is too small. Sure can." He ruffled up my hair and walked out to the garage.

After he got it working again, I took it up to my room and found colorful paper in my desk. I started punching holes and soon had a pile of colorful confetti covering my desk. I borrowed a jar from my mom's canning cupboard to hold all the confetti. Soon the jar was half full.

I paused my project on Saturday because my mom brought me a massive list of chores. On Sunday, I had most of the church bulletin punched before my mom noticed the growing paper pile on the pew and pinched my leg. But on Monday, I brought my project to school and asked Miss Lee if I could keep it at my table and punch more confetti during free time. She said it would be fine, if it didn't become a distraction to the other Friend Bears. By Wednesday, two other girls had jars of confetti on **their** tables! I'm a trendsetter!

I pulled a pink sheet of paper from the garbage and started punching more confetti for my jar. *This is going to be a great day. Maybe I'll start a new club called "Paper Puncher Pals," only **everyone** will be welcome in it, and there won't be a stupid secret* *signal.* I couldn't help smiling as I dug through the garbage looking for colorful scraps of paper.

"What do you think you are doing?" Wendy and three other girls stood around me as I hung upside down on the monkey bars. I started coming out for recess again after I became a trendsetter. I haven't worked up the nerve to start my "Paper Puncher Pals" club yet, but my trend of confetti in a jar has spread through the class like wildfire.

I stared at her and said, "I'm doing a flip if you'll move over a bit."

Wendy scowled and put her hands on her hips. "No, Penny, I mean **why** are you **copying** the Kitty Cats with your **lame** jar of confetti," she hissed.

WHAT!? My leg slipped, and I grabbed the bar with my hand to steady myself. I could feel my heart pounding in my chest.

"Yeah, Penny, Wendy started those jars for The Kitty Cats, so you shouldn't be copying us since you're **not** in the club," said a tall girl, who I think is called Sheila and isn't even in our class.

I dropped to the ground and faced the group. My hands shook from anger. "Wendy did **not** start the trend, **I** did!"

Wendy sneered and stepped closer, her spit hitting me in the face as she screeched, "I did so! Everyone knows it, and you are a copycat, **not** a Kitty Cat."

LIAR! ATTENTION-STARVED LIAR! I looked around at the unfriendly faces and shouted, "The Kitty Cats is the stupidest club with the dumbest name, and only losers would want to be in it!"

Wendy laughed and pointed her finger at me. "The only loser here is you, Penny." Her club members bobbed their heads and smirked.

I stared at them, unable to formulate more words. I pushed past the barricade they formed and stomped into the school building. Still fuming, I went to my classroom, grabbed the jar of confetti, and threw it in the trash. I winced as the glass broke, and all the colorful bits of paper sifted to the bottom of the trash can. Exhausted, I collapsed in my chair. I buried my face in my arms and silently cried. *I wish I never left my cozy hideout, teachers' restroom.*

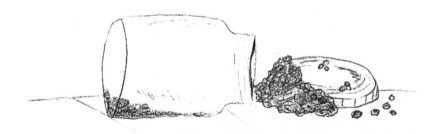

~TEN~

APRIL SHOWERS BRING MAY FLOWERS, SOMETIMES

Thirty days! It is thirty days until my birthday! My double-digits birthday! I am planning a Hawaiian luau birthday party, and I am going to invite all the girls in my class. We will have pineapple upside-down cake, flower leis, and yard games. And if it ever quits raining, my dad is going to build a hut with tiki torches in our backyard! I already designed invitations. Mom agreed to let the girls sleep over after the party; it will be the best birthday **ever**!

I think even my mom is excited. She took out the sewing machine and began laboring over a Hawaiian *muumuu* for me to wear at the party. She cut out the pattern and material with no trouble but kept ripping out all the stitches she sewed. *I hope she has it done in thirty days.*

My dad has wood and hay to make the hut, but he says May is a long way off, and there is enough time for hut-building. I am getting nervous it won't happen. Each day I tell him where we are on the count down. I remind him how fast his thirty-five years went, and that's **years** not **days**! I don't seem to be getting through to him because the hut is still a pile of lumber.

I found a box of old seashells from my parents' honeymoon on Sanibel Island and used them to decorate my invitations. I dusted off the calligraphy set I bought at a garage sale and began writing each invitation by hand, with a personal message in calligraphy. Each one took me almost an hour because of my terrible handwriting, but they are fantastic. I am anxious to give them out, but Mom said I should use better etiquette and wait until one week before my birthday.

"We should make grass skirts at the party!" I shouted at my mom during breakfast.

She jumped and dropped her coffee mug which was, fortunately, almost empty. "Penny, when will you learn to use your indoor voice?" She dabbed at the coffee soaking into the tablecloth. "And, Darling, where will you get all the grass?"

"I can cut it from the field across the road," I said confidently. "Daddy has those hedge clippers; I can cut a lot at a time."

Mom sighed and rubbed her forehead. "I don't know, Penny, it sounds like a lot of work." She got up to refill her mug. "I guess if you are willing to gather the grass, I will research it at the library and learn how to assemble them."

"It won't be too much work. You'll see!" I ran over and hugged her before hopping up the stairs to get dressed.

Later that afternoon, I ran to the car when Dad got home. I yanked open his door and said, "Give me your clippers. I only have a couple of hours before dark!"

Dad raised his eyebrows and chuckled. "I wish I had half your imagination, Penny Pie." He lowered his voice and looked around, "Are you sure hedge clippers are your best weapon against…you know who?"

I rolled my eyes. "No, Daddy, I need them for an **important** project," I shifted my feet impatiently. I took a deep breath and explained my skirt idea to him. "And," I concluded, "there are two hours left of daylight. If I haul along my red wagon, I can fill it up with grass before Mom calls me in for supper."

Gathering grass was harder than I thought. Dad made it look easy, but the clippers were heavy and awkward to handle. Most of the grasses were dead and matted together. I found green patches, but those were impossible to cut too; they bent between the blades of the clippers. I ended up ripping the grass out of the ground by hand.

Mom's dinner bell rang, and the only thing I could show for my efforts

was blistered hands and a wagon not even half full.

As I dragged my wagon up the driveway, I reminded myself it would be worth it. My party was going to be the best Hawaiian luau birthday anyone ever had.

~ELEVEN~

IT'S NOT A PIG ROAST, ROGER

The week before my party, it was warm and sunny, and everyone seemed to have extra energy at recess. I hung upside down on the monkey bars, watching the former Kitty Cats argue over who copied whose outfit. Their club disassembled with the balmy weather because no one wanted to hang around inside the tornado slide, and they couldn't think of anything else to do at their meetings.

Limited on my monkey bars tricks (my hands were still blistered and bandaged), I spent most of recess dangling upside down. Wendy walked over to me (after winning the outfit argument) and flared her nostril, "What's with your hands?"

I turned my upside-down head toward her. "Oh, nothing, just calluses."

Wendy smirked and flipped her hair. "Well, I'd give up the monkey bars if it made my hands look like **that**."

I gave a fake yawn, pretending the conversation bored me. "Yeah, I guess." I considered telling Wendy about the skirts but decided not to. I grabbed the bars, winced, and jumped down. "Hey, in case you forgot, my party is in one week, and it's a sleepover."

Wendy rolled her eyes, "Didn't forget, you talk about it **all** the time."

So would you if you were having the world's best Hawaiian luau birthday party. "I hope you can come." I felt my armpits get sticky with sweat as she stared at me.

"Yeah, I'll probably come." She gave me a disdainful look before heading back to argue more with the former Kitty Cats.

I looked around for someone else to talk to, but everyone looked busy. I wandered over to the tires and practiced leap-frogging without using my hands until the bell rang.

I sprinted toward the blacktop, enjoying the feel of warm air blowing my hair around. It was finally long and straight enough to whip around in the wind. As we gathered into our class lines, I tossed my hair over my shoulder, closed my eyes, and smiled up at the sunshine.

Four days before my party I was (as my mom put it) a basket of nerves. *Everything must be perfect!* I delivered all my invitations days ago, and I wrote reminder notes to all the girls today during free time, in case they forgot. Wendy said she was going, and the other girls usually copied her. Becky, Danielle, and Susan said they were coming too. Priscilla couldn't come because it was her weekend at her dad's. I even invited the new girl, Charlotte, who moved to our school in April. She told me she would have to ask her grandma, but she was pretty sure she would say yes.

Roger asked if we were roasting a pig, then he *oinked* at me during recess. *Poor Roger, I'd feel dejected too if I were left out of the* **world's best** *Hawaiian luau birthday party.*

Three days before my party, my dad finished the hut and stuck two tiki torches in the ground on either side of it. Mom finished my *muumuu*. It looks good from a distance. Up close, you can see little holes where she ripped out stitches, but I am sure with my grass skirt covering it, the holes will hardly be noticeable.

I decided to wear a different colored silk hibiscus in my hair each day, as a reminder of my party. And today for Show and Tell, I talked about the Hawaiian flower. "The hibiscus is the state flower of Hawaii," I told the class, stroking my almost permless hair.

When the bell rang for recess, I skipped all the way from the blacktop to the monkey bars, holding my hibiscus securely in place with my hand. My cuts and blisters had healed. I swung from rung to rung, enjoying the sun on my skin. A voice below startled me causing me to miss a rung.

"Seriously, Penny, are you part monkey or something? Why are you always on those bars?" Roger, dressed in a stretched-out

Scooby-Doo T-shirt and too-short shorts, stared up at me, a sarcastic look on his face.

I felt myself stiffen as I stared back at him. *You are such a dweeb.* "Roger, don't feel bad because you aren't invited to my party. It's girls-only."

Roger snorted. "Why would I want to go to your pig roast anyhow?"

I closed my eyes and counted to ten, fighting the urge to stick my tongue out at him. "It's not a pig roast, Roger, it's a Hawaiian luau, but you probably don't know what that means," I explained coolly.

Roger pushed up his nose, "*Oink! Oink!*"

I clenched my teeth but kept swinging. *Roger, you are incredibly unclever.* "Who knows," I quipped, "maybe next year I'll invite the whole class." *I won't invite pig-boys though.*

"Whatever, Penny, maybe I'll be too busy. Nice napkin in your hair, by the way!" He awkwardly galloped away, *oinking* and laughing.

I kept swinging on the monkey bars until the bell rang. I tried somersaulting down, but my legs tangled, and I fell. "*OW*!" I screamed as my head slapped the gravel. I sat up, dazed for several seconds. *Oh please, don't let anybody see me.* I looked around to make sure there were no witnesses. Something wet trickled down my temple. My hand trembling, I reached up to find my silk hibiscus gone and a bloody gouge in its place. I found my smashed purple flower and stuffed it in my pocket. I stood up but had to sit back down as the playground spun around me. I waited for a couple minutes, then slowly rose and staggered toward the school building.

My class was already inside. I darted into the girls' bathroom, threw my ruined hibiscus in the garbage, and shook the dirt from my hair. I gasped at my reflection in the mirror. My hair was matted with drying blood, and more seeped from the wound.

I tried using the scratchy brown paper towels to soak up the blood, but they were less than absorbent and made the blood and dirt smear. Taking a deep breath, I plunged my head beneath the faucet, wincing as the water hit the gash, trying to rinse my hair the best I could. I dabbed at my hair with a paper towel and trudged to class. I casually sat down as if nothing happened.

"Penny, you are late. Do you have an excuse, or should I mark you tardy?" Miss Lee asked without looking up.

"Sorry, Miss Lee. No, I don't have an excuse." I slouched in my seat, keeping my head down, staring at the math worksheet on my table. I pretended to focus on fractions but couldn't help hearing the giggles.

"Hey, Penny, what'd you do with your napkin?" Roger whispered.

I squirmed as Wendy leaned closer. "Seriously, Penny, what's with your hair? Did you **wash** it in the **bathroom**?" She looked horrified.

"Miss Lee! Penny's bleeding!" Danielle shouted.

I slouched even lower in my chair and vigorously attacked my fractions.

Susan turned in her seat and stared sympathetically. "Penny, what happened to you," she whispered.

Miss Lee clapped her hands sharply. "Class, it is silent work time, which means I should be hearing only silence. Penny, come here, please."

I shuffled to Miss Lee's desk with my head still down, trying to lean the bloody side into my shoulder. Miss Lee pushed my hair back and exclaimed, "Penny! Did you get injured at recess?"

Obviously. "Not really, it's just a scratch." I cupped my hand over the gouge, as if to prove my point.

Miss Lee gently moved my hand away so she could get a better look. "Oh, Penny, that looks terribly painful. You poor thing." She patted my cheek. Her hands smelled like the lemon soap my mom uses, and suddenly I felt homesick.

She shook her head. "Penny, why didn't you come to me sooner?" she asked. "That's a deep cut. You better go to the nurse's office right away." She gently pressed a soft tissue into my gouge and gave me a hug before walking me to the door.

Miss Lee cared about me. My heart lightened as I looked at her sympathetic eyes. "Thank you, Miss Lee." *Thank you.*

I walked the familiar path to the nurse's office and plopped down on her cot. "Goodness, Penny, we are getting to be good friends, aren't we?" She smiled softly as she cleaned and bandaged my head.

*Friends? Yeah, right, like I have any of **those**.* I studied her freckles as she gently taped the last bandage. "Thanks," I managed to mutter.

"Why don't I show you the teachers' restroom. It's a nice place to freshen up." She stood up and held out her hand to me.

"Thank you, that would be nice." I smiled and took her hand. Even though it was babyish, I held it all the way to the door. She guided me down the hall to the teachers' restroom, where I faked unfamiliarity. She showed me the vanity and handed me the brush. I saw a few of my own hairs stuck in the bristles.

After she left, I sat for a few minutes and brushed my hair until it was smooth. I opened the drawer and pulled out the perfumed cloths. I took my time wiping them up and down my legs. I stared at myself in the mirror, thinking how she called me her friend. Then I meandered back to my math sheets, trying to ignore my pounding headache. I avoided eye contact with Roger and Wendy and quickly finished my fractions. I drew hibiscus flowers around the answers until the rest of the class finished math.

Two days before the party, I organized the grass into kits with yarn and zip ties. Mom couldn't find instructions for the grass skirts, so we improvised. Dad had the idea to use zip ties to attach the grass to the yarn, which seemed to work. I completed a skirt, and I was right, it hid the holes in my *muumuu*.

I made extra *leis* in case the girls wanted more than one. The
new girl, Charlotte, said her
grandma gave her permission to
come, as long as she met my
parents first and they didn't seem
crazy. That brought my total to
six (counting me), the perfect
number for games.

The day before the party, everything was perfect, except for the
pineapple upside down cake; it was a flop. My dad took it to work for
lunch, and my mom baked an angel food cake instead. "Fresh
strawberries and whipped cream will be even tastier than pineapples,"
she told me as she pulled the cake from the oven.

I didn't agree, but I said, "Sounds delicious," because she
seemed frazzled over the party.

Before bed, I opened my bottom dresser drawer and gathered
my friendship bracelets. I danced out to the Hawaiian hut and nestled
bracelets on top of each grass skirt kit. *Perfect.*

Dad came out and set up a card table outside the hut for the
cake and gifts. He moved the grill closer, so he could serve the burgers
next to the cake. Burgers weren't very Hawaiian, but I was glad he
wasn't roasting a pig. Roger would never stop *oinking.*

My dad headed into the garage while I stood in the Hawaiian
hut for several minutes, admiring my beautiful party. When Mom

called me in for bed, I ran to the garage and said, "Thank you, Daddy, for the best hut ever!" I grabbed his neck and hugged him tightly.

He laughed and hugged me back. "You're welcome, Penny Pie. I hope it's your best birthday ever. It's hard to believe you're turning twenty-one already."

I squealed and swatted his shoulder. "Oh, Daddy, you're silly." I gave him another squeeze and said, "That's your last nine-year-old hug."

"Well, I better have one more!" He hugged me close and kissed the top of my head. I danced back into the house, smiling and thinking how things were changing. Somehow, I didn't feel like a kid anymore. Ten seemed different, more grown up. Tomorrow I would be double digits. More importantly, I would be hosting a party that would make me popular. *Finally, popular!*

When I got upstairs, I brushed my teeth and put on my white cotton nightgown. After I brushed my hair 100 strokes, I snuggled into my covers and fell asleep thinking about my friendship bracelets. *Tomorrow, I will finally give them all away!*

~TWELVE~

IT'S MY BIRTHDAY!!!

On my birthday, the school day dragged on forever. Making matters worse, I couldn't focus on anything but my party. I was daydreaming about my tiki torches when Miss Lee apparently asked me a question. "She means you, Penny," Danielle whispered and poked me in the ribs.

I sat up straight and said the only words my mouth could form, "Tiki torches." The class erupted in laughter as I slunk down in my seat burning with shame.

After school, I ran up to my room, put on my *lei*, and pinned my grass skirt in place. I glanced at the clock. *3:00. Only one more hour until my party!*

After checking and re-checking everything for the party, it was finally the countdown. *Only fifteen minutes more!*

"Darling, you are making me terribly nervous with your pacing around. Why don't you go help Daddy outside?" Mom shooed me out of the kitchen.

I skipped out the door and across the yard to the hut for a final check. The card table had the cake, strawberries, and whipped cream already on it, along with two gifts. My bracelets, *leis*, and grass skirt kits were still in place. The tiki torches were lit and the grill smoking.

Dad stood at the grill, scraping it with the grill brush. I hopped over to him. "Do you have enough burgers?"

He rubbed his chin. "Well, let's see. I have ten meat patties. Three for me, four for your mother, and half each for the six little birds." He smiled and turned back to the grill.

I sighed, "Daddy, I'm serious. I don't want to run out of food."

He winked at me. "I've got it covered, Penny Pie. I promise to stuff you all full as little piggies."

I rolled my eyes and skipped back inside to make sure my mom had the prizes ready for the yard games. She shooed me right back out, so I plopped down on top of our picnic table, where I could clearly see the driveway. *This way, I can see the first car as soon as it pulls in.*

I straightened my grass skirt and adjusted my *lei.* Then I smoothed my almost-straight hair and checked to make sure my pink hibiscus was fastened tightly. My stomach quivered with excitement. *Any minute now my first guest will arrive!* I stared anxiously down the driveway.

At 4:10, I tried not to panic, but many things ran through my mind. *Why are they late? What if there isn't time now to do all the yard games before dark? What if the whipped cream melts before we can eat it? What if the burgers start to burn because they are on the grill too long? What if I forgot to give directions?*

"Penny," my mom asked softly. She stood behind me, holding the prize box, a concerned look on her face.

"What," I mumbled, not bothering to turn around.

"Darling, you did write 4:00 on the invitations, didn't you?" She sounded doubtful.

"Yes." I nervously twisted my *lei* with my finger and glanced at the driveway. *Any minute someone will drive up.*

Mom sighed and patted my shoulder. "I'll refrigerate the cake until your friends arrive."

"No! They will be here any second," I snapped.

Mom shook her head, walked over to the hut, and set the box on the card table. She whispered to my dad, while he grilled the ten meat patties. I could hear them whispering back and forth but couldn't tell what they were saying. I returned my focus to the driveway and tried to listen for cars.

At 4:20 no one had arrived. I sat on the picnic table, pretending to focus on the driveway, hiding my tears from my parents. I told myself Wendy and the rest of the guests were coming. *I don't know what the delay is, but they are coming.*

Relief washed over me when I heard the phone ring. *Directions! Maybe I* **did** *forget to add them to the invitations! They are calling for directions, I'm sure of it!* I wiped at my face and ran inside.

I rocked from foot to foot as I watched my mom

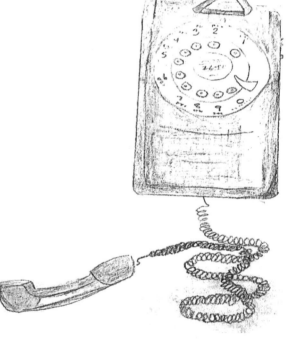

twirl the phone cord around her fingers with one hand and click her nails on the finger wheel with her other hand. She looked at me expressionlessly as she rested the receiver between her ear and shoulder. *Why isn't she giving directions?* She mumbled under her breath, shook her head, and hung up.

Mom took a deep breath before speaking. "Darling, I'm sorry, but that was Mrs. Simms. Wendy isn't feeling well and won't be coming. She said Becky is staying with them this weekend and feels she ought to keep Wendy company."

I felt like puking. *WHAT? That is a lie! Wendy is a liar! She's trying to ruin my party!* "Did anyone else call? Why aren't the rest here?" Desperation swept over me.

"I don't know, Darling, are you sure they were planning on being here?" She looked tired.

I'm not sure about anything. "They **said** they were coming." Tears threatened to spill over, and I turned my face away from her.

"Well, Daddy can keep the burgers warm, and I'll put away the rest of the food until they arrive."

At 4:45 the phone hadn't rung again. I sat alone on the picnic table, tears running down my face, my nose one big ball of snot. I laid down on the table and sobbed. Every part of me hurt. It was worse than when I fell off my bike and skinned my knees in the gravel. That kind of pain wasn't as bad.

My classmates didn't care, so neither would I. *I don't care. I don't care about any of them. I don't care about my stupid birthday or my dumb games or my ugly grass skirts!* My dad came and sat on the picnic table beside me. He rubbed my back, not saying anything because there was nothing to say. *I am not popular. I will **never** be popular.*

After I cried it out, I left my dad sitting alone on the table. I trudged up to my room and crawled into bed with my *muumuu* and grass skirt still on. I kicked my legs as hard as I could against my bedspread and shouted, "Loser! Loser! Loser!" I don't know who I meant, them or me. I started ripping petals off my *lei* and wiped my nose on my pillowcase. *Who cares. Who even cares!* I was about to shout again when I heard voices in the kitchen. I heard voices that weren't my parents in the kitchen! I jumped out of bed and almost tripped down the stairs.

My mom beamed at me and motioned me into the room. "Penny, darling, this is Charlotte's grandmother, and, of course, you know Charlotte." Mom waved me closer.

Charlotte smiled shyly. "I'm sorry we are late, Penny. My grandma doesn't know the streets very well yet."

"Poor Charlotte is at the mercy of this old lady trying to find my way around a new town. Happy birthday, Penny!" Charlotte's grandma embraced me in a big, comfortable, grandma-type hug. I stood motionless for a few seconds, trying to realize what was happening.

"Thank you! I…I'm glad you are here," I stuttered.

Charlotte handed me a beautifully wrapped gift with a big bow and tiny hibiscus flowers drawn on the wrapping paper. "Happy birthday, Penny."

I stared at the gift, overcome with happiness. "Thank you," I whispered and took a deep, wobbly breath. "Come with me!" I took

Charlotte by the hand, and we ran outside to the Hawaiian hut. I set her gift on the table and showed her the *leis* and grass skirt kits.

Charlotte looked around at the amazing party my parents had put together. "My old school was huge, and I was always going to parties, but this is way cooler than any of those."

I sighed, "I wish I were popular enough to always go to parties."

Charlotte tilted her head and peered at me. "Why?"

For a minute I stared at her, trying to articulate all the reasons. "Because…I…well…because…" *Why* **do** *I want to be popular?* I couldn't think of a single reason. The whole thing, trying to force people to like me, seemed silly. I started laughing until I was holding my stomach and crying. Charlotte joined in, and soon we both were sobbing with laughter.

"You are strange, Penny, but I like you," she shook her head and dried her eyes.

We had the best evening playing all the games I had planned. I gave Charlotte the entire prize box, even though I won some games. Dad made perfect burgers, and there was plenty for us to eat. The angel food cake **was** better than pineapples. We squirted so much whipped cream on top of our pieces, they were completely buried.

After we finished eating, I opened my gifts. My parents gave me a neon-green windbreaker and a big box of craft supplies, including a fancy new paper punch.

Charlotte gave me a cloth-covered diary with yellow and purple hibiscuses on the cover. I had never owned a diary, but I already knew what I would write about first: the world's best Hawaiian luau birthday party and my new friend Charlotte.

We saved the grass skirt kits for last. I looked at all six piles and said, "Let's make one giant skirt to hang around the hut."

Charlotte laughed and said, "That sounds fun." When we had used up all the grass I worked so hard to pull, we stood admiring our giant skirt. Charlotte tilted her head and said, "Let's tie on all the *leis* to make it more colorful."

"That is a perfect idea," I smiled at her as I grabbed the pile of unused *leis*.

When we finished, my dad helped us hang it around the Hawaiian hut. He took a step back, admiring our work. "I never saw the old hut dressed better." I didn't even roll my eyes at him. I love his silliness.

I looked at all the friendship bracelets and wondered what to do with them. Then I had an idea. "Charlotte, would you like a friendship **necklace**?"

As Charlotte and I laid in our sleeping bags on my bedroom floor, I told her what my school year was like before she moved here. We laughed over all my trips to the nurse's office and my awful book report. I showed her how to make colorful confetti, and she promised to teach me how to dribble a basketball. She said she liked my Care Bears sleeping bag, and I said I liked her elephant slippers. I showed her my olive-green suede leather jacket, and we both agreed nothing smells better than suede. And somehow the sting of being teased lessened.

She laughed a lot but was also serious. She told me about her parents dying when she was young and what it was like living with her grandma. I listened to her talk about her old school and what it felt like to move away.

We imagined what we would do over summer break and made plans for our next sleepover. We stayed up later than I ever have and finally fell asleep as the first rays of sunshine peeked into my bedroom.

Dear Diary,

Some people are destined for popularity. I am not one of them. Neither is my best friend, Charlotte, but that is fine with us. We both turned ten last spring and will start fifth grade soon. Even though my best-ever summer is almost over, I'm not sad at all. I know fifth grade is going to be brilliant.

About the author

Laurie Pluimer has written for multiple magazines and her local newspaper. *The Year of Penny* is her debut children's novel. She resides in Wisconsin with her husband, two children, one dog, and two cats, and a duck. You can find her hiking in the woods or on Facebook at **Laurie Pluimer Books**. Learn more at **lauriepluimer.com**.

Made in the USA
Monee, IL
23 June 2023

36694169R40050